Mother Tree

THE CHOSEN ONE

ANDRE REDMOND

Illustrations by Lyle John Jakosalem

To order additional copies of this book, contact:
Xlibris LLC
1-888-795-4274
www.Xlibris.com
Orders@Xlibris.com

Well here is another day full of sunshine. My name is Michael and I'm going to see Mother Tree today. She is a very old and special tree. No one knows how old she really is and she will not tell you either. One thing she will tell you with great joy is a story. She will capture your heart while you listen.

3

I work so much these days that I only get a chance to see her twice a month. No matter how bad I'm feeling at the time, after I hear one of her stories I always end up with a smile on my face when I say goodbye to her. Finally, I'm here! "Hello Mother Tree."

"Hello Michael," Mother Tree responded, "Nice to see you again, just flop down and have a seat somewhere."

"Okay," so I sat on a log and made myself comfortable and then Mother Tree began with her story.

Well this story begins long, long, ago with an Indian chief named Raging Horse. He had a daughter named Little Flower. Little Flower was very beautiful and she had a smile that would soothe your soul. Little Flower was an adult now and ready to get married.

There were two warriors Raging Horse said that had enough honor and courage to marry his daughter. So Raging horse decided that by the next full moon Little Flower will choose her husband. Little Flower was happy because she liked both of the warriors. One of the warrior's names was Running Spirit and the other was Silent Hawk. Both warriors were very handsome which also pleased Little Flower.

The next morning as the sun was rising the two warriors jumped on their horses and started leaving to hunt for deer. They wanted to show Little Flower that they were good hunters, so she would have clothes to wear and food to eat. Little Flower went along to watch them hunt. They tied their horses to a tree and then went up a hill.

As soon as they reached the top of the hill they saw a herd of deer! Silent Hawk and Running Spirit started going down the hill slowly trying not to make a sound.

They found a good position and then Running Spirit and Silent Hawk aimed and one by one, shot their arrows at the herd of deer! Running Spirit shot six deer, while Silent Hawk only shot four.

Little Flower was very pleased with the both of them. So pleased in fact that she said, "We will bring all the deer back to the village and I will cook for both of you."

On the way back they were all very hungry, Running Spirit and Silent Hawk had food but Little Flower forgot to bring hers, so Running Spirit and Silent Hawk gave her some food. Little Flower said, "thank you to the both of them." Little Flower and Running Spirit was almost done eating their food when she noticed that Silent Hawk was not eating.

Little Flower asked, "How come you're not eating?"

Silent Hawk answered, "I gave you all of my food."

"Why did you do that," Little Flower questioned.

Silent Hawk said, "you were hungry and I wanted to make sure you were full."

Little Flower smiled and responded, "it would not please me if you did not eat anything, please eat the rest of my food," Silent Hawk said, "okay."

When they arrived home Little Flower told her father Raging Horse all about the hunt and that she would prepare a meal for the warriors. She happily prepared the deer meat and cooked it just right. After she served the meal and they all finished eating Silent Hawk and Running Spirit thanked Little Flower for the food. Little Flower decided she wanted to dance so Raging Horse said "play music," and everyone danced.

Raging Horse smiled, he was very happy to see his daughter laughing and having a good time with Silent Hawk and Running Spirit. The dancing ended but conversation did not. After a while everyone was tired especially Little Flower and so she told everyone goodnight and went to her teepee. Not long after everyone else left too.

"That was a very fun dinner," Little Flower thought to herself before she fell asleep.

A few days later it was cloudy and windy, so Little Flower thought of a little test for the warriors.

She found Silent Hawk and Running Spirit and told them "one day I may go into the forest and not be able to find my way back."

"I'm going to hide in the forest and I want the both of you to find me. Walk around the camp four times and then come look for me." The warriors said okay.

Silent Hawk and Running Spirit walked around the camp four times as instructed and went out to look for Little Flower. They both noticed her footprints in the dirt but they didn't agree on which way she had gone. Silent Hawk and Running Spirit went their separate ways to look for her.

Little Flower was patiently hiding under a big tree waiting for the warriors to find her. Almost twenty minutes went by and then she noticed Silent Hawk walking towards her and saying "I found you."

"Took you long enough," She responded smiling. They talked while they waited for Running Spirit to find them. Running Spirit came about ten minutes later.

"I may not have found you first, but I did find you," Running Spirit huffed as he was out of breath from running.

Little Flower smiled and responded, "well maybe the two of you found me but can either of you catch me?"

Little Flower took off running and laughing. While she was running she fell down.

"I think I hurt my ankle," She cried.

Running Spirit said "see if you can walk on it." Little Flower replied, "I will try." Little Flower started limping as she walked. Silent Hawk and Running Spirit walked beside Little Flower to catch her if she fell. Silent Hawk saw that she was struggling and wanted to help her, so he said, "Hey Little Flower, I will carry you."

"And so will I," Running Spirit added.

So Little Flower got on Silent Hawk's back and they started on their way home. Almost halfway there Silent Hawk was tired so Running Spirit said, "I will take over." Running Spirit carried her the rest of the way home.

When they reached the camp Running Spirit let Little Flower down slowly.

Little Flower kissed Running Spirit on the cheek and said, "you are very strong thank you for carrying me the rest of the way home." Then Little Flower turned to Silent Hawk and hugged him real tight and thanked him for carrying her too. Little Flower started to walk away real fast. Silent Hawk and Running Spirit looked at each other baffled.

Running Spirit yelled," Hey Little Flower, I thought you hurt your ankle."

Little Flower just laughed and said, "It feels a lot better now! Thanks for the ride."

Silent Hawk said to Running Spirit "she tricked us," and with a sly grin Running Spirit responded, "lets' get her."

Little Flower started running and laughing while they chased her all around the camp. They finally caught her near the lake so Silent hawk and Running Spirit smiled at each other and looked at the lake. Little Flower said "what are you two smiling for?"

Then Silent Hawk grabbed her arms and Running Spirit grabbed her legs and walked to the lake. Little Flower said, "No, No, No, No, No! Wait!" Before Little Flower could finish her sentence they threw her into the lake. Running Spirit and Silent Hawk laughed and started walking back to the camp. Little Flower crept up behind them and yelled "We are all getting wet today!" She grabbed Running Spirit and Silent Hawk by the back of their pants and pulled them into the lake. They all laughed and played while splashing and dunking each other under the water till the sun went down.

A few days passed and Little Flower told Silent Hawk and Running Spirit to get their horses and take a ride with her into the woods. She said "I have a gift for both of you." They rode to the woods, tied their horses to a tree and started walking into an opened field. Little Flower pointed towards a tree and said, "look behind it; your gifts are there."

Silent Hawk and Running Spirit went behind the tree and saw two bows, twelve arrows, and two satchels. Little Flower said, "each of you will get a bow, six arrows, and a satchel. Very soon the full moon will come and I will choose which one of you I want to be my husband. I made these gifts to let you know that I am very pleased with the both of you."

"Do you know which one of us you want to be your husband?" Running Spirit asked.

"Yes Little Flower do you know?" Silent Hawk added.

With a bright smile Little Flower said, "you both will find out when the full moon arrives."

While they were talking they didn't notice that a bear had walked towards the tree. It was getting dark so Little Flower suggested going home, and as they came around the tree the bear let out a loud growl and started to run towards them.

"RUN," Silent Hawk screamed.

As they were running Silent Hawk and Running Spirit were putting an arrow in their bows. Silent Hawk had his arrow set in place and turned around to shoot the bear, but the bear was right in front of him. The bear swung fast with his right paw and then his left, striking Silent Hawk in the face and knocking him to the ground. Silent Hawk's face started bleeding.

Running Spirit shot the bear in the side with an arrow. The bear growled and faced Running Spirit. He shot the bear again in the stomach and the bear stumbled. At that moment Silent Hawk got back up and shot the bear in the heart with an arrow and the bear fell down and died.

Little Flower said, "I'm glad you two are ok," and went to Silent Hawk to mend the wounds on his face. When she was done they all heard a sound, almost like babies crying. Just then two little cubs came out the woods and ran to the bear crying.

Little Flower said, "Now I know why the bear attacked us; she thought we were going to hurt her cubs. We will raise her cubs and when they are old enough we will set them free." Running Spirit and Silent Hawk agreed and they all went home.

Silent Hawk went to see the medicine man about his wounds. Six days later the medicine man came back and said to Silent Hawk, "you will have scars on your face, three on the right and four on the left, there is nothing more that I can do."

Sad and disappointed Silent Hawk put his head down and started to shake his head and said to himself, "Little Flower will surely pick Running Spirit now."

Finally it was the night of the full moon. Raging Horse spread the word for everyone to meet. The two warriors were standing side by side. At that moment everyone was waiting on Little Flower to come out of her teepee. When Little Flower came out she looked very beautiful. She walked to her father and said, "I wish mother was still alive to be with us tonight."

With a loving and encouraging smile Raging Horse said "your mother and the Great Spirit are smiling on you tonight, now go and choose the one you love."

Little Flower went in front of the warriors; the crowd was waiting with anticipation. Little Flower said, "I choose Silent Hawk!"

The crowd cheered and yelled their congratulations.
Running Spirit said, "good luck to the both of you."

Silent Hawk was amazed, he said "Little Flower why did you pick me?" I love you very much, but I didn't think you would pick me."

With a gentle smile Little Flower explained,

"When I was hungry you gave me all you had to eat and when you thought I was hurt you offered to carry me first even though Running Spirit carried me most of the way home. You see Silent Hawk it's the little things you do that also matters, with time my beautiful face will fade away and only the wrinkles will remain, but you my love you will not even notice them. You didn't fall in love with my beauty, you fell in love with my soul, your face might be scarred but your love is never ending, so that is why I chose you."

Silent Hawk kissed Little Flower and said, "There will never be a day that goes by when you will ask yourself if I still love you because every time you look into my eyes you will know that I do."

Raging Horse was very happy and smiled.

He said "Everyone! Please dance, sing, and enjoy. Tonight we celebrate the union of Little Flower and Silent Hawk."

"Wow Mother Tree" Michael said, "that was a beautiful love story."

Michael turned to the two men sitting on the log, "did you guys like the story?"

"Yes" said Bobby "I liked it very much." Aaron said "I liked it too, hopefully one day I can find someone who loves me just as much as Little Flower loved Silent Hawk."

"I'm sure you will, Aaron," said Mother Tree. "Well, until we all meet again be good and take care of yourselves."

One by one they each said, "we will Mother Tree goodbye."

Mother Tree smiled and said, "Goodbye boys."

Written by: Andre Redmond

Edwards Brothers Malloy
Thorofare, NJ USA
May 7, 2014